The Apatride
and the Confused Dog

Predrag Humphrey Mihajlovic

EnglishTranslation by
Avison Communication AB
www.avison.se

© Predrag Humphrey Mihajlovic 2017
Förlag: BoD Books on Demand, Stockholm, Sverige
Tryck: BoD Books on Demand, Norderstedt, Tyskland
ISBN: 978-91-7699-550-1

The Apatride and the Confused Dog

One: The Apatride

All of a sudden he starts to shake with fever, and is forced to stay in their home.

It feels odd. The odd thing is not just the suddenness, but that this is the first time he's been ill since he began wandering. It's true that illness or injury is far more hazardous to the solitary person than to one who is not — as you're forced to get by on your own – yet during his wandering years he's begun to think of solitude as a form of immunity against illness. The brain refuses to let the body fall ill for fear that there is no one to help.

But now, after such a close encounter with two people, his brain has begun to relax for the first time in ages, letting the body fight back instead.

'Let the body fight back!' says the brain.

He's also had a stroke of luck. He's no longer alone. The unusually kind and tranquil siblings help him get into bed and give him a cover.

It has always been important to me, he thinks with his eyes shut as he senses sleep slowly beginning to ease over him, to not catch an illness that doesn't let you fight back. I've ended up in, and yet I've also created, a world that both exists in parallel and intertwines with the great big world, which is no more real than the parallel one. I'm aware of that. My world has substance, it's no illusion. It's not empty! Had it been empty, I would have been sick. I would have been stricken by an illness that I would not have been able fight back against.

How can he be sure that his world is not an illusion? Well, he's met thousands upon thousands of others like him.

There are more and more of us now. We are a reality! It's just that I've distanced myself from them, physically. My ego will not let itself be categorised! It is my weakness and my strength alike.

He had snuck into the house the evening before. The storm was so fierce that not even the dense forest could shield him. The house was actually a cottage. He would not have entered had he known that it was not abandoned. The door was unlocked and he entered without knocking. They were sleeping and could not hear him. And he could not see them because it was pitch black. All he could do was shut the door behind him and lie down on the floor next to them.

Come morning they found him asleep, curled up on the thin, faded and large doormat. They were neither particularly afraid, as he was sleep, nor surprised, as there was nothing odd about uninvited guests turning up after a storm like that. When he woke up they were quickly able to find a language they all spoke. His name was Danilo, and his hosts Julia and Oliver offered him a cup of hot tea and a couple of crisp breads with blackberry jam.

He was a wanderer. He walked alone, without so much as a dog to keep him company. He then explained that he observed the world and the things that went on in it, but kept himself aloof from it. Nor did he think of himself as some kind of witness. He never carried paper and pen. But sometimes he would use a chunk of brick to inscribe a thought or two on someone's fence, or on a tree or roadway, just in passing. Danilo also said he wanted to be alone, which was not to say that he hid from people: he went and spoke to people when necessary and responded to them if they came and spoke to him. It hadn't always been that way, but that's the way it was now. It didn't bother him now, just as it hadn't bothered him when things were different.

He told them that he was a slow walker, that he could cover long distances on foot and that heavy shoes were no inconvenience. In three years he had never once been in a hurry, which explained why he had been caught out in the storm and had to walk through it for a few miles before making it to the nearest residential area.

"The thing that matters to me is to never get where I'm going."

He had no passport, but was able to move freely from one state to another.

"How do you manage that?" asked Julia.

"Don't ask," said Danilo. "I'm very crafty sometimes."

Magic tricks and illusion came in handy.

One day three years ago, he said, his country had been erased from the world map.

"Erased?! How can that be?"

"It's true that I'm a magician, but only truly mighty magicians are able to pull off a thing like that."

That's why he decided to leave.

"If I can't be there, then I intend to be everywhere," he said at last.

After that, Julia said that she and her older brother had been living in the cottage for more than three years. She said they lived there alone and that it suited them. It was interesting, she said, that he had been wandering for as long as they had been staying put in the cottage. That's why the pair of siblings expected to hear him tell them a little more about himself.

But Danilo said nothing. He had said precisely as much as he considered necessary. After finishing his tea he stood up, intending to be on his way. He was a wanderer who never stayed anywhere for more than one night.

But that's when he started trembling with the onset of a sudden fever that forced him to stay.

He has finished another cup of hot tea, and now lies covered in two blankets. A strange woman's pale blue eyes are observing him; kindly, but he sees an unusual twinkle in them. And they're beautiful.

Everything around him looks beautiful and pleasant. Everything around him feels good. Only he is unwell. He hears the front door open. The sound is hardly perceptible, but he still hears it. Julia's face breaks into a gentle smile. The sound was her brother Oliver leaving the cottage.

"Oliver has left to go on his daily morning walk," she says.

She places her left hand over Danilo's forehead and notes that the fever seems to have subsided.

"Is it afternoon already?"

"No, it's still morning," she answers.

Danilo finds her voice pleasing. He wants to keep hearing to it, and hopes that she can read the wish in his eyes. It appears that she can. She continues speaking in a whisper:

"I have only Oliver and he has only me. There is no one else in this world for us. We need each other equally much. Both of us need solitude too: he because of his fear, and me for my writing."

Danilo feels the heat rising in his body. Julia speaks almost uninterruptedly, and to him it sounds almost as if she is singing. He would like to know more about her writing, but he is afraid she might think it presumptuous, so he bites his tongue.

But she does not pick up on his secret wish, and keeps talking about Oliver instead:

"My brother is scared that someone might stab him at any moment. He's someone who has never been able to resist anyone or anything. Last time he was injured so badly he nearly died. Each time something happened he was the victim of unhappy circumstance. It's true! But he still thinks it was all carefully staged and it's impossible to convince him otherwise."

"But how is he doing now?"

"He's doing better now, as we live here alone. His fear has almost disappeared. We haven't spoken about our past lives since moving here; Oliver doesn't want to and I manage to avoid it for his sake."

They hear Oliver entering the spacious cottage. He enters the room and says he forgot his glasses. They are on the windowsill. A soft smile still plays on Julia's lips, but she is no longer speaking. Oliver slowly pulls a handkerchief out of his trouser pocket and stands there for a moment wiping his lenses. Then he leaves the cottage again.

Danilo is no longer trembling. He is on the verge of falling asleep. He cannot recall the last time he felt so exhausted. Julia steps away from his bed and leaves the room. He shuts his eyes.

Somewhere between wakefulness and sleep, Danilo thinks:

The absolute present! And everything is uncertain because of it. Whether it will turn out like in a story or like in real life he does not know. I've been wandering three years now. I myself am afraid of certainty – the finished story. Just as I carried the fear with me in my old life, I carry it with me today as well. It's just that the fear is different now – I wouldn't want to be rid of it. It's the fear of the end's nearness, of narrative finality, of the end itself. Whatever is certain can bring me to the end. That's why you have to walk slowly! No crossroads! That's my inner imperative.

Why, he often reasons, should I free myself from this new fear when it lends me strength in my struggle against the old one?

Each time he confronts this question, his faith only grows that the persistence and strength of the new fear make him hardier. Though he hadn't been able to blot it out when he needed to do so, he'd at least been able to transform the old fear into the new one.

I don't want to become someone else. I just want to live with the new fear, the more fitting one, he thinks. It's the way he's thought for more than three years now. The same person, liberated by the content of the new fear!

Yet everything proceeds through Danilo's constant self-coercion, his well-rehearsed awareness of a structure. It's very easy to find an example of this in a seemingly banal event that occurred recently.

At the time he was getting more and more tired of the constant trekking. His body was about to give up. As he was about to pass through a big city in who knows what country, he forgot for a moment that he was walking aimlessly. He forgot that what he wanted to avoid was haste. It was a mild night with a clear sky, and the street was empty when he spotted a light blue bicycle flung down on the pavement. It was a large city, so he was uncertain whether he would be able to make it out before dawn. He made it as far as the bicycle and picked it up. After a brief inspection he could tell that it was functional: the handlebars were in good shape and the chain and wheels appeared to be unharmed … He looked the bicycle for a moment, then the road ahead. With a feeling of joy, he thought that this simple contraption would be able to carry him 300 miles at least. Assured that there was no one nearby, he got on the bicycle and started riding. He rode faster and faster. But after just three minutes he turned around and looked back at where he had started from. He looked again at the empty, tidy street ahead of him, then back at where he had started.

In three years I have never covered so much distance so quickly, he thought.

Realising this made him so queasy that he almost fell off the bicycle. Once he had gathered himself, he slammed on the brakes and got off. He walked back slowly and returned the bicycle to where he had found it. Then he turned around slowly and ambled away. Now he felt calmer.

This is when Danilo realised that he himself would be the most difficult thing and person of all to over-come on his way to freedom. Because if he had felt a spontaneous need to make it somewhere on time, even if only for a moment, it meant that the sense of responsibility was still in him. The fact that the inner voice was still in him somewhere was not merely a matter of habit or of his inherent nature; it also meant that the old fear had not left him entirely, that it had not been fully transformed into the new one. Because his sense of re-sponsibility was so bound up with the old fear. Because his sense of responsibility was also bound up with his love for something that had not existed for a long time. It had been a dead weight that he'd felt again and again these three long years. Everyone should feel responsi-bility, but only if they were able to make a difference; or if everyone were able to feel love for something – that's what he used to think. He thought it was im-possible now. Danilo believed that his power lay in the lack of responsibility.

He has been lying with his eyes closed for an hour, yet without falling asleep. He turns over on his back and fixes his gaze on the ceiling. He has been wandering for three years now and has grown unaccustomed to doing anything else. But this doesn't bother him; what would bother him is being forced to do something.

It's not as if his body has gone soft with idleness. On the contrary, his years of travelling on foot have given him endurance. His body is lean and wiry. But he's not thinking of his body. He's thinking of something else. He's happy that he is able to stop thinking at any moment just when he has started thinking of anything at all. He's happy that he can stop doing something he has just started on. He's happy that he can suddenly start doing something he hadn't meant to do at all, and which there is no need to finish.

He turns his head towards the door. It stands open. Julia might be in her room writing. Oliver may still be on his walk in the forest. Where there are no knives. Danilo doesn't know what Julia and Oliver are actually doing right now. He hears soft steps and knows that they are Julia's. She walks into the room and sits down on the edge of the bed. Her face no longer wears the slight smile it did before, but is radiating a peculiar joy.

Danilo turns his head toward the wall and fixes his gaze on the clock. It's 12 o'clock. The month is September, the year 1995. No, it's October 1995.

"I think one thousand two hundred days have passed since my brother and I moved here," says Julia as she rises from the edge of the bed.

Danilo is lying on his right side, looking at Julia. She wears a light blue hooded sweatshirt and a pair of sweatpants. She has her hands in her pockets and is crossing the room with a masculine gait. She is not exactly tall.

Actually she is quite short, but she has a beautiful figure, he thinks.

"That's a long time," he then says, "to constantly stay in one place, at least for me."

"But maybe there isn't such a big difference between wandering and standing still."

"Maybe ... you know, we're sitting in the same room," says Danilo.

"What did you do during your wandering years?"

My wandering years are still going on, Danilo plans to say, but then holds back. No need to be so pedantic and ruin her eagerness.

"Wandering means not doing anything. All you do is walk," he says, feeling vaguely dissatisfied with the conversation.

"Okay," Julia says eagerly, "Now I want you to listen carefully and help me. Divide the number of days I said by five!"

"All right, done."

"How many days did you get?"

"Two hundred and forty."

"Exactly. Now find the difference between this number and 500, and multiply the result by five!"

"One thousand three hundred if I did the numbers right," Danilo replies.

"You just figured out the number of days I've planned to stay here," says Julia in a euphoric whisper.

"I have a quite a long time to go."

"Yes, that makes three and a half years to go."

"What is it all about, if I may ask?"

"Nobody knows but Oliver, but it's really no big secret. And now you know the first half of the story."

"So tell me the other half."

"There's so much to tell, and yet it can be told in just a few words," she says, settling again at the edge of the bed.

"May I hear the words?"

"I write short stories. Every five days I write a new one. That's all."

"A tough job, am I right?"

"Sometimes it is very tough, but it gives me great pleasure, and everything is going as planned, which is very important to note. My plan is to create a collection of 500 stories. One to two pages long, not more. I'm nearly halfway through now. I just finished my two-hundred fortieth story, and I wouldn't say that my joy is any the less for the fatigue I feel. Nobody would object to this kind of fatigue … Have you ever tried to write anything? Tell me!"

"Once upon a time," Danilo answers thoughtfully and with a smile tugging at the corner of his mouth, "I wrote poetry in high school and university. I thought some of them were very good poems. Even in front of my friends, I must now admit, I was at pains to give the impression of being a true poet. Today it's been over five years since I've written anything."

"I've never published anything, but I do intend to. Have you had the chance to publish anything?"

"Only very little, just two or three poems in a local literary journal. To be honest I've never thought of myself as a poet. It was just a bout of youthful enthusiasm."

"Oliver is my greatest support. He's my personal critic, which gives me the strength to go on. He reads what I write by day in the evening, and in the morning I patiently listen to his impressions and his opinion. It's true that I never edit what I've written, but I do make use of his comments in the next stories. He says that walks in the forest and reading my stories make him more stable. And truly, as the days and months go by it seems to me that he is doing better and better, that Oliver has actually regained his health. We have settled into a routine, and that makes us feel more and more secure."

"It's very nice hearing you speak," says Danilo. He expects a response, but she doesn't react to his words in the slightest.

There is a brief and spontaneous lull in the conversation. Julia is looking somewhere above him, but not into the distance. The happiness is still written on her face. As he watches her, it seems to him as if she is absent in some way. Her eyes shine and are no longer those of a stranger. Maybe all the unknown things surrounding her are, but here and now, and so close to him, she is no stranger. The thing that perplexes him a little is the discrepancy, however slight, between the content of the story she tells and the emotional remove he hears in her voice. He tries to imagine her face while she is writing, but doesn't manage to. Try though he might, he just can't call forth the image in his mind. He gives up.

The next moment he is lying down with his head resting in his right palm as he continues watching her. She lets him.

But the lull in their talk lasts only an instant, and Danilo breaks it with a question:

"Why didn't you stay where you were and try to write?"

"Just like Oliver, I needed to be alone."

"To me it seems as if you were alone there too."

"We weren't alone there, says Julia, but we did feel alone. Here we actually are alone but we don't feel alone."

"Don't you have any close relatives?"

"My mother died three years ago."

"And your father?"

"Oliver remembers him, but I don't. My father simply disappeared before I reached an age where I would be able to form a memory of him. My mother had always avoided mentioning him, and I don't remember if I ever asked about him ... His absence had no impact on our material welfare ... Do you think I had a peculiar upbringing?"

"Well, it wasn't like the one I had at least."

"What was yours like?"

"Most of my life went the way it was supposed to. Or at least the way people thought it was supposed to go back there and back then. And it would have been great if it had kept going that way."

After hearing Danilo's answer Julia returns the subject of her mother.

"My mother was blind for the last two years of her life," she says, and then begins to talk about it, her mother's blindness. She says that its onset was not unexpected. That it had been lurking in the background for years, and that she and Oliver had known about it. "One morning five years ago, my brother and I woke up and were told that our mother could no longer see us. She was sitting in her usual chair at the kitchen table when she told us she had woken up blind. At first she had not been aware of what had happened. She thought she had woken up in the middle of the night and that the reason she couldn't see anything was because it was dark. But it did not take her long to realise what had happened. We were more frightened than she was." Julia goes on and tells him that her mother asked them not to worry about her, as she had been making preparations for this day for a long time. Her preparations consisted of measuring the distances to all the places she used to spend time in or visit. She counted her steps and wrote down the distances in a notebook. She pored over the notes she made and eventually memorised all of them. She categorised all the distances into two groups. In the first group were all the recorded distances between her bedroom – which she had fixed as the hub of all her movements – and all of the other rooms in the house. For example, the distance between her bedroom and the kitchen was 14 steps, including all the turns to the left or right she needed to make. In the second group were all the distances between her bedroom and all the places she went that were outside the home." Julia tells him about another proof of her mother's preparations for the onset of blindness: the pair of black glasses and the white cane she had acquired a few years before it happened. Her mother also asked Oliver to get a guide dog (at that time he had just recovered from his injuries from his second stabbing, but had not yet begun to suffer panic attacks). The dog was big and black and was named Cesar. During the warmer months of the year our blind mother would go on long walks with Cesar. She didn't let us join her. Cesar made us forget that mother was blind. She felt absolutely safe in the company of her guardian dog. But she spent the majority of her time in the bedroom, which had now also become her living room. In there she used to listen to books on tape while Cesar lay on the floor dreaming. We read her the newspaper every morning at breakfast. I was 18 then. Oliver was four years older than me." Julia wraps up her story by saying that one day, not long after going blind, their mother did not wake up. Her dog Cesar died a short time thereafter.

Danilo makes no comment.

"Where are your parents now? Are they doing well? Do they believe you will return? Did they ask you to stay? Was the separation painful?" She showers him with questions.

He starts to answer, but suddenly he pulls her in towards him and gives her a kiss. She accepts it.

"It is time for lunch," she says and leaves.

He tracks her with his gaze until she disappears from the room.

"How do you get food?" she hears his voice say.

"There's nothing to it," he hears her voice say.

It's after lunch and Danilo is seated in an old wooden chair outside the cottage as he thinks back on one of his best friends. His friend's name was Jordan. Danilo's memories of him are coming back in a flood – fragmentary and out of chronological order, but his brain quickly pieces together the unforgettable four-year story of their friendship.

At the same time he observes the woods around him, fixing his gaze on a narrow road he hopes leads into the city.

But what does it matter where it leads? It doesn't matter at all!

Then he returns to the cottage, but does not close the door behind him. Julia has finished writing her story. He hopes she has fallen asleep.

She must be fast asleep now, he supposes.

Peering into the kitchen from the little boxy hallway he is able to see Oliver stretched out on a little bench. Actually, he can only see his feet, which are clad in unusually thick socks.

He must be fast asleep now, he supposes.

He goes into his room and searches for his thick but shabby dark brown leather jacket. He finds it under the bed and puts it on very quickly. He feels impatient, and his movements grow ever faster. He finds a pack of cigarettes in the jacket's upper inside pocket. He feels around in it for a cigarette using his index finger. It's empty. No cigarettes! He's gripped by something close to panic, then fumbles around feverishly with his finger once more.

"No, there's one more," he whispers to himself with relief.

He tiptoes out of the cottage. For a moment he suppresses his initial urge, and sits back down in the same place. He lights the cigarette, takes a few deep drags, then tosses it onto the damp greenish brown of the forest floor. He gets up slowly and stamps it out for safety's sake. At length, he begins to make his way resolutely towards the narrow road he had been gazing at a few minutes earlier.

Now he's walking along a forest road like something out of a fairytale, leaving the swaying ferns behind him. It's as if he called them to life and these sleepy sylvan plants are now waving him farewell. It's not the twilight hour, but the darkness of the forest makes it feel like twilight.

Great, he thinks in an attempt to convince himself, now I can walk the rest of the day and all through the night. I won't find a place to sleep until early in the morning.

Now Julia and Oliver, those two endearing, hospitable and humble people, enter his thoughts.

"I have to do this," he whispers. "If I don't leave them now, I may get the urge to stay on forever." Yes, he thinks, they will have forgotten me by tomorrow. And you know what, I don't care in the least if they wonder where I've gone without saying thank you and goodbye. I came unexpectedly, and I'll leave the same way.

He is firmly convinced that he is leaving this hidden, forgotten place forever. He's done the same thing countless times before. But he had rarely ever lingered in any one place as he had in this one. He would like to think that he is experiencing the same feeling he did when he left everything behind three years ago.

He thinks: When a person is carrying the load, he walks quickly so that he can put it down at his destination as soon as possible and unburden himself. But I feel relieved of all burdens, and now I'm walking along at a slow pace again. I feel set free from all the memories of the time I was hurt. It's nicest to leave without saying goodbye. Back there, all that was just a silly, innocent meeting. An encounter not worth remembering!

Suddenly a bird flares out of the underbrush behind him, and the road ahead rears up as if it would reach to the impenetrable grey sky. Nearly in the same instant, both road and sky disappear. He doesn't even have time to register the narrow road rushing up and smacking him in the face. Complete darkness falls around him.

Two: and the Confused Dog

It takes eight hours before Danilo comes to the conclusion, as he wakes up for the second time, that he was probably knocked unconscious.

The first time he woke up he didn't wonder what had happened, as it did not occur to him that anything had happened in the first place. In the beginning he didn't recognise the room he was in. Eventually he was able to recognise some of the objects around him, but was unable to put them in context. Once he finally recognised the room he was in, he thought he had awoken out of his fever. He tried to get to his feet, but a sharp pain in his head thrust him back into unconsciousness.

Now he is awake for the second time and knows that something, at least, has happened. The throbbing swelling in the back of his head explains a lot, if not quite enough. He opens his eyes and looks for the clock facing left, but only spots it when he turns his gaze to the right. Now he understands that everything he saw after the first time he woke up had been rotated by one hundred-and-eighty degrees.

It must be that way, he thinks, I've never been unconscious before, and it looks like that's what happened this time.

Julia enters the room and says:

"Looks like you're back again. I've been in here a few times, and each time you're either fast asleep or talking in your sleep. You even vomited once."

"I don't understand," he says, "and I expect a good explanation from you and your brother."

"You're not getting a good explanation from me. We just found you lying on the road not far from the cottage, and that's all."

"Is that all?"

"Yes, and now it's time to take another pill for your headache. And remember: as far as Oliver is concerned, you were feeling sick and just fainted. And you don't remember a thing."

And Danilo doesn't remember a thing, it's true.

"I don't remember anything, it's true…but how did you find me?"

"If he gets the idea that you were attacked," she continues without responding to his question, "he will end up in a state that I shudder to imagine."

Danilo spends the next two hours sleeping. After that he wakes up and continues to lie there as the hours pass, watching as the sun peeks out or disappears behind the clouds floating high above the forest.

After fourteen hours, he sits down in the chair outside the cottage without observing or contemplating anything in particular. It seems as if he has recovered, but he still feels safer sitting down.

So he sits. The same memories as yesterday.

It's the last hour of the morning. Oliver returns from his regular walk, draws near Danilo and smiles.

"I'm wondering if you feel up to talking to me for a little bit?" he asks courteously, sitting down on the ground beside him.

"I do, yes," replies Danilo. "Go ahead!"

Oliver remains quiet for a moment, then says:

"Can you feel the autumn in the air?"

"Yes, I can."

"So you know about that, huh?"

"What do you mean, knowing the smell of autumn?"

"No, I don't think you need a particularly good sense of smell for that. I was thinking about this art, this magic, whatever you call it."

Danilo glances at him, then fixes his gaze on the trees in front of him.

He and Jordan were different in many respects. Jordan was a real genius, the best student of his generation, while Danilo had been average and with significantly less ambition than his friend. But they had absolutely no doubts about each other, and spent time together without discussing their academic performance. The same went for money: whenever Jordan didn't have any, Danilo did, and vice versa. Danilo studied law, and Jordan studied physics. Like most young people, they dreamt of changing their home country someday, once they were finished with their studies. At the same time, they enjoyed the lifestyle they had back then and did not want their study years to end so soon.

"I guess I do know a bit about it," Danilo finally replies to Oliver's question, "but I rarely make use of stuff like that, only when necessary."

"What are the tricks?"

"I can't give you a good answer to that."

"Show me some," says Oliver with zeal in his voice.

"Why should I? It's just an illusion!"

"But please, I'm terribly curious," Oliver says even more ardently, then adds: "I think people sometimes need to be deceived. That's less dangerous than deceiving yourself."

Then came the accident. Like all accidents, it was sudden. It was a hallucination in the form of a black flock of birds flying directly for his eyes. Jordan suffered a nervous breakdown and became severely unbalanced. The fact that everyone must die one day can be regarded as a consolation. Death is inevitable and comes for us all, but not everyone is condemned to suffer such a malady, so when it strikes it is a tragedy greater than death.

"Okay," he says, "would you please fetch me those two boiled eggs? They're right over there, barely a meter from you."

Oliver is about to say that it's impossible for there to be any boiled eggs nearby, but that's when he sees them.

"Those really are eggs," he says, fetching them. "How were you able to know that they would be boiled, too?"

"That doesn't matter. Will you let me continue?"

"Of course! Of course!"

"In that case, go ahead and check which one is hardest!"

Oliver strikes them against each other, but neither one cracks.

"What sort of eggs are these?"

"Try again! One of them definitely has to be harder."

"Look, I'm hitting them again and again! And nothing is happening!"

"Weird, right?"

"Weird!"

In the beginning, Danilo and all of Jordan's loved ones were hoping that he would make a recovery, and that in time the young man would laugh at his own hallucinations. During the few weeks he spent in hospital he was visited by at least two or three relatives or friends each day. He himself was often in such a good mood that it felt as if the whole episode would soon be ancient history.

"Aren't you strong enough to crush an egg?"

"It looks that way! What kinds of eggs are these anyway?"

"Toss them," says Danilo, "those aren't eggs, just two perfectly ordinary white rocks."

"How did you do that?" asks Oliver, laughing as he lets the two white rocks fall from his hands. "Tell me how you did it."

"I only did what you asked me to."

"But how?"

Danilo remains silent for a second or two.

But Jordan's condition is getting worse and worse. Fewer and fewer people come by the hospital, and more and more time passes between their visits. Apart from the few that visit, in the end there are no more visitors. Danilo is starting to realise that his friend is well and truly lost, but he continues to fight for his friend's dignity with a remarkably naïve optimism. He sees a faint trace of hope in Jordan's wish to pass his final exams. He is refused entry to the university exam hall, so Danilo starts a campaign for Jordan's rights. He even sets up a meeting with the dean, but his appeal to compassion goes unheard. They don't accept his claim that there is no harm in awarding a mentally ill person his bachelor's degree.

"I just wanted it to happen that way," he replies.

"Who taught you that?" asks Julia's brother.

"No one. It happened by itself."

"How many years have you had this ability?"

"For as many years as I have been wandering. And it was odd for me too. But I chalk it up to the known rule that every evil carries within it the seed of something good. If somebody offers me a better explanation than that I'll accept it."

"Everyone ought to wish for this ability," says Oliver. "If only I could do it three times in my life! Or at least once, the time it's needed most."

"I don't abuse my power," he says, "except when it proves necessary in order to cope with my existence."

"I have to admit that I feel safe with you."

"You're really pleasant and friendly."

"I'm neither more pleasant and friendly nor more unpleasant and unfriendly than anyone else."

"Oh."

On the very day he indignantly left the dean's office, Jordan disappeared. The search for him turned up nothing. Danilo grew more and more convinced that Jordan was no longer alive. But then a thought occurred to him that would have a decisive influence on his life a few years later when he decided to commence his endless wandering. If Jordan chose death by disappearance, maybe it was no death at all.

That's what he thought back then. And it's what he thinks on occasion even now.

Danilo spends the rest of the day alone. He doesn't do anything and doesn't move from the spot. But he doesn't know what boredom is like. He just lies there for a spell. He keeps his eyes shut for a while, then opens them. For a fraction of a second he asks himself:

Who knocked me unconscious?

But the question lingers only a wink of an eye before it is gone forever. He survived the experience. Other considerations were nothing but unnecessary bother for the brain.

He knows that people like him cannot have enemies. Or friends either. It's sad, but that's the way his life is nowadays. He couldn't care less. There are plenty of roads in front of him – one road picks up where another leaves off. He has melded all of his roads together into a single stretch – the great road, yet without depriving others of their own roads.

"It's a great big world anyway, with room for everyone," he whispers.

He notices that his hair has grown long. He gets up from the bed, finds a pair of scissors in the bathroom, and starts cutting. He also cuts off his beard and then shaves. He gives himself a look in the mirror. Now he looks a bit younger and better groomed.

"I think I'm better looking too," he says out loud to himself, jokingly.

He hasn't tried to talk to Julia nearly the whole day, except for a brief moment after lunch. She has been standoffish too.

Maybe she feels hurt because I tried to leave them in such an unseemly way. Danilo then thinks: To her it was sheer escapism, while for me it was a natural act. Maybe she saw it as an insult, but for me it was something of a relief.

"You have made a nice recovery," she says at dinner. "So do you feel up to continuing your wandering?"

Danilo can't be bothered to respond to Julia's suggestive question. It occurs to him that Oliver may have asked him the same thing at lunch.

"Who knows if we'll see each other again tomorrow," she adds. He can't actually detect any sarcasm in her voice.

In spite of the tone of her statement, Danilo still suspects that her words might mean her hospitality is at an end.

Or maybe she expects some kind of response from me, he thinks.

In any case, he doesn't respond to this question either.

Anything I say can be a shackle on me, he thinks.

Oliver remains quiet the whole time, as if he weren't there, but Danilo notices that he is in good spirits.

"Is it really true that you've never stayed anywhere for more than a few days?" Oliver suddenly asks.

"No, that's not true," Danilo replies, darting a glance at Julia. "It was the beginning of my wandering days. I don't know how I ended up at a centre for people like me. There were lots of us there, and we came from all over the world. The people assigned to take care of us were really nice. They were reverent too, no doubt about it, except that they were too much so, as if we were children. Many of us liked it."

"But not you," says Oliver.

"But not me," Danilo confirms before going on: "All of us were given the opportunity to learn a new language, but we also had the option to do basic knowledge refreshers."

He pauses for a moment, smiles and then says:

"Our hosts were courteous. If one of us started writing, for example, these friendly people would come up and practically hold the poor guy's hand and guide it to help it write better. It bothered me, so I left the centre after barely a month."

It sounds like a very funny story, Oliver says – though maybe the part about the hand was a little bit exaggerated – and struggles to keep from laughing out loud.

It's a new day now. Danilo sits down in the same chair outside the cottage at the same time as yesterday. Feeling great, he gazes out into the unknown. He doesn't put his brain through the effort of even the least bit of laborious thinking. He just sits and sits, taking in the smell coming off the mouldering leaves.

And then, at the same time as yesterday, Oliver returns from his regular walk through the forest. Wearing the same smile as yesterday, he approaches Danilo. Again with the same decorum as yesterday, he asks to have a little talk and sits down on the ground beside him.

"The weather is the same as yesterday," he says, "and it smells of autumn like yesterday."

"Yes, everything is repeating itself."

"You've been in my thoughts without interruption ever since yesterday."

"It would be better if you had bent your mind on something else," says Danilo, "but thanks all the same."

"This is the first time I've met anyone like you."

"That should come as no surprise, considering your social life over the past three years."

"I mean that in all seriousness."

"All right, then I accept your remark in all seriousness."

"It feels like you're someone who can be trusted."

"Then that's a good thing, for you and for me."

"It means nothing to you, right?"

Danilo makes a face to signal that he doesn't know what answer he prefers to give.

"I'm talking about danger. I'm talking about fear," says Oliver.

"The risk of danger is always there. The question is the degree to which it is manifest. Fear is in all of us. The question is whether we can live with it, whether we can handle it."

"You're honest," says Oliver, "but don't worry, your words don't hurt me. Julia once spoke to me that way too."

"My intention was to defuse the conversation."

"I intend to get straight to the point," exclaims Oliver, cutting through the air with his left palm.

"As you should," says Danilo with a smile.

"I want to say…you should know…to my mind fear is always legitimate, even if you object that my fear…the fear I feel is a figment of my imagination."

Danilo nods slowly.

"No, you don't understand me. You're taking the wrong person seriously."

"What do you mean by that, Oliver?"

Oliver does not respond, and says:

"Sometimes I want to disappear."

"But still exist, right?"

"Exactly!"

"Don't think you're the only one who wants to have it that way," says Danilo, more to himself than to Oliver.

"If I disappear, then the fear disappears too."

"Then this is the right place for you, I dare say."

"Maybe, but something needs to happen! It's necessary!"

"That's premature, my friend," says Danilo, again more to himself.

"Just wish it!"

I'm not sure I understand him, Danilo thinks. We're talking about different things: Oliver has become entangled in the local, while I have been thrust into the global against my will...ha ha. Plus I still know almost nothing about global matters. But there's plenty of time left for me to start learning.

"Sure, but what?" he then asks.

"There must be something!"

"Oliver, I'm an apatride."

"What? What's that?"

"An apatride is someone who has no citizenship. A stateless person. I'm not an apatride in the true sense of the word. Actually I decided to become like one, and more than just that. I don't want to be active in any way. I don't want to influence or be influenced."

"I would love to be able to do that, to influence."

"Influence? I don't understand how you can expect anything of the sort in the midst of this isolation."

And there the conversation ends. They walk slowly into the cottage.

"I'm going out now to take a walk," says Danilo after lunch.

He can see that Julia is in a better mood than yesterday. She is barefoot and is wearing only shorts and a short-sleeved shirt.

She says that she would love to come along, but that she has a strong urge to get some things down in writing, that ideas for stories are just flooding in.

Oliver darts a quick glance at his little sister.

"Would you please come back in half an hour? I would like to have a word with you."

From the door Danilo answers:

"Sure Julia, I promise."

She's so spontaneous, he thinks. She speaks to me as if we've known each other a long time.

After half an hour he's back. He walks into his room. Julia is in his bed. She smiles, and he understands that she is naked beneath the covers. He stands next to the bed, waiting patiently for her to say something.

"We have to be quiet," she says, "otherwise we'll wake Oliver."

Danilo climbs in and settles in close. Her body is warm, and her eyes shine with an unusual intensity.

A short time later she gets out of bed, dresses quickly and leaves the room without saying a word.

Early the next morning she's back in his bed. He's awake. He went to sleep early last night.

"How long do you intend to stay?" she asks.

"I can leave at once," he replies with a little smile. "If I have to."

"I didn't mean it that way. I'm asking because I'm worried. My whole body trembles when I think that you won't be here in a day or so."

"What am I supposed to say now?"

"Just tell me when you plan to leave us."

"In a day or two, I don't know."

"Plus one more day after that."

"How's that?"

"Promise me that you'll stay one day longer than you planned."

"But I haven't definitely decided which day I'll be leaving."

"So decide, and then add one more day!"

"Okay, let's say any day then, plus one day."

Two more days pass.

Danilo enjoys his time in the siblings' company, but he doesn't like the orderliness in their home. Oliver takes his walks in the mornings, sleeps in the afternoons, and reads his sister's stories in the evenings. And every five days, like Julia says, her next story is waiting on the desk. She spends mornings and afternoons in her room. Her nights she spends in Danilo's room. And Danilo sits outside the house until lunch, takes a walk in the afternoons, and spends his nights with Julia. She is in his thoughts all the time, and it feels good.

"Are you ready for a morning walk?" Oliver asks him.

"Of course I am," he tells Julia's brother.

Now they are pacing along the narrow road leading into the city, or which may lead into the city. Then they turn off the road they're on and walk deeper into the sleepy forest.

"Has Julia told you about our mother and father?"

Danilo is silent.

"She must have told you something?"

"Yes, your mother went blind and then she died."

"It goes without saying that my mother's death was a difficult experience for us, but I'm thinking of something really terrible that happened before we came here. Something that in fact led to her death. Something that hastened her death."

"Your sister hasn't mentioned anything about that."

"I certainly understand that, because it was a shock to her. Seeing one's father for the first time after so many years, and in such a state, it was terrible! I was six years old when father left us. My sister didn't remember him, she only had a few photos to look at. Those two photos were the only thing that let her form a picture of him in her mind. Why he left us? I don't know. Why he came back after nearly fifteen years? I don't know that either. But he did come back. He turned up out of the blue! And he shouldn't have done that. Julia and I were out when it happened. If we hadn't forgotten to lock the door, I'm certain that none of it would have happened. Mother was in her bedroom as usual, and Cesar was lazing about on the floor by her bed. Cesar!"

"You're not going to say what I think you are, are you?"

"That's right," Oliver confirms as he slowly wipes off his glasses. His eyes remain fixed on the ground after he puts them back on.

"What a horrible thing to happen," says Danilo, slowing his pace more and more. "So unbelievable and so tragic! I'm speechless."

"The irony of fate! To end your life in the house that you once owned, to be savaged by the jaws of that house's dog, it just can't be described in any other way," says Oliver, folding his hands and fixing his gaze on the forest floor.

Danilo nods.

"Julia got home a few minutes before me..."

Danilo nods and says:

"Poor Julia."

"Yes, I don't think it's necessary to describe what she experienced then."

The next day Danilo rises early, convinced it will be his last in Julia's and Oliver's home.

I definitely don't belong here, he says to himself as he walks into the toilet, where he takes a shower and brushes his teeth. Then he walks back to the room and sits down on the bed. He sits there for a while.

I've never been in Julia's room, not even once, he thinks.

Danilo remembers her saying the other day that Oliver thought it best if no one entered. He remembers wondering whether what Oliver said was meant ironically or if there was something more serious to it. He remembers not being able to make heads or tails of it. And he remembers not asking her about it either.

What did she mean by that? What did he mean by that, he wonders.

For a moment he intends to enter her room while she is sleeping, but then dismisses the thought.

Julia is probably sleeping now, relaxed, on her back, her hands resting atop her head.

It's true that she seems unusually pretty, attractive, and charming to him, and it feels totally natural to be with someone like her: someone who has found herself.

But I have to be off! What would I do here if I were to stay? What would it mean, to stay here? Is this the spot of my disappearance? Is there any such spot? Doesn't it mean: disappearing is like being everywhere and nowhere at once?

He lies down on his back and peers at the window. The leaves and time itself stand still.

She has her room. I haven't been there. That's the room where she writes her stories. Does she think that she doesn't exist to other people when she's at it? Her writing. Does she think she's disappeared all these years since the awful thing happened, all these years she's been writing, and will continue to write?

The leaves and time itself stand still.

And me, he wonders, what about me? Would I ask a question like that if I had been in love? No, I'm not in love with her! I have to leave this place for good! Today! I've made up my mind, this is the way it's going to be!

"Why are you so sweaty?"

"I didn't know you were awake," he says to her, startled.

"Why are you so sweaty?" she asks again, mimicking the way Little Red Riding Hood asks questions of the wolf disguised as her grandmother.

"I'm not sweaty, I just took a shower," he says.

"Say: Because I want to look attractive."

"Because I want to look attractive," he says in the voice of the disguised wolf.

"Good!"

"Shall we go to your room? What do you say to that?"

A sunbeam makes its way through an opening in the treetops, shines decisively through the little window pane and lights the plank floor directly between them, creating a theatrical atmosphere in the room.

"I don't know why Oliver asked this of me, but I promised him that no one will enter my room. And a promise is a promise."

"Okay, I have to talk to him about this today. It all sounds so childish. Oliver can't persuade me otherwise."

"Then you can read my stories!"

"All of them, I want to read all of them!"

"It wouldn't take so very long."

"And what if I just read one a day?"

"I don't dare entertain such hopes," Julia says as the sunbeam vanishes.

Danilo enters her room after lunch.

"You're leaving us today, right Danilo?" Oliver had asked him in the morning, before going on his inevitable walk.

"Yes I will, without a doubt…but would you mind if I visited Julia in her room to say farewell?"

"It's not up to me. I'm not the one who can forbid such a thing. I just don't recommend doing it."

"I know, and I take sole responsibility," Danilo says ironically.

At first he doesn't see anything unusual in the room. It's very sparingly furnished: a sofa, a green desk, two black chairs, and empty blackish green bookcase and nothing else. After that he spots a small fireplace on his right. In the fireplace he sees what must be a hammer.

An empty bookcase?! A hammer?! Danilo wanders at what he is seeing for a few seconds. When he glances at the window he sees a motionless squirrel staring intently at him.

Julia is seated at her desk. Her hair is combed back and she is wearing glasses. She looks sleepy. There is a white handbag to the left of her on the floor. On the table is a thick notebook with a red leather cover. He sees no typewriter. And no pen either.

She says timidly:

"Welcome, Danilo. How nice that you finally came!"

"Thanks. I agree," he says, wanting to add that this is his first time seeing a squirrel even though he's been here for a few days; but he bites his tongue.

"Don't you want to read my stories?" she asks, picking up her notebook with both hands and holding it out towards him.

"Of course I do. Then you can read them to me. I like hearing you speak."

Danilo opens up the notebook and finds a thin light green pen in it. He slowly turns the first page, as it bears no text. On the second page it says in handwritten letters: Story Number 1. He assumes the story starts on the next page, so he turns the page. There it says: Story Number 2. On the next page it says: Story Number 3. He skips ahead at random. Nothing. Just blank pages. He doesn't have the courage to lift his gaze from the notebook and look at her.

"Now what do you say?"

The squirrel quickly vanishes behind the trees.

"Impressive," Danilo says without looking at her, placing the notebook hesitantly on her desk. "You'll have to read me one of them sometime."

He musters all his strength and looks her straight in the eyes. Now he cannot see that the little squirrel has returned again. Now he cannot see tension in the playful animal's eyes.

"Do you want me to go ahead and read one to you now?" she asks excitedly. "How about I start with Story Number 13?"

"No, start with the first one and read to me for as long as you are able," he says and sits down in the chair opposite her.

"I feel so tired," says Julia as she slowly slumps over the table, nodding off at once.

Danilo stands up and walks over to her. He kisses her on the forehead and then on the cheeks.

"Sleep well," he whispers in her ear before settling back in the chair.

The leaves and time itself stand still. The squirrel has vanished again.

Now she's asleep, slumped over the table, and he's sitting there waiting for her to wake up. And when she wakes he won't leave her. He doesn't know how long it will take, but he'll stay for as long as necessary.

"Plus one more day after that," he whispers to himself.

Or: now she's asleep, slumped over the table, and he's sitting there waiting for her to wake up. And once she's awake he'll leave her. He doesn't know how long it will take, but he'll be on his way as soon as he can.

"Plus one more day after that," he whispers to himself.